I'm Going To READ!™

These levels are meant only as guides;
you and your child can best choose a book that's right.

UP TO 50 WORDS

Level 1: Kindergarten–Grade 1 . . . Ages 4–6
- word bank to highlight new words
- consistent placement of text to promote readability
- easy words and phrases
- simple sentences build to make simple stories
- art and design help new readers decode text

UP TO 100 WORDS

Level 2: Grade 1 . . . Ages 6–7
- word bank to highlight new words
- rhyming texts introduced
- more difficult words, but vocabulary is still limited
- longer sentences and longer stories
- designed for easy readability

UP TO 200 WORDS

Level 3: Grade 2 . . . Ages 7–8
- richer vocabulary of up to 200 different words
- varied sentence structure
- high-interest stories with longer plots
- designed to promote independent reading

MORE THAN 300 WORDS

Level 4: Grades 3 and up . . . Ages 8 and up
- richer vocabulary of more than 300 different words
- short chapters, multiple stories, or poems
- more complex plots for the newly independent reader
- emphasis on reading for meaning

LEVEL 3

Library of Congress Cataloging-in-Publication Data Available

2 4 6 8 10 9 7 5 3 1

Published by Sterling Publishing Co., Inc.
387 Park Avenue South, New York, NY 10016
Text copyright © 2005 by Harriet Ziefert Inc.
Illustrations copyright © 2005 by Dale Gottlieb
Distributed in Canada by Sterling Publishing
c/o Canadian Manda Group, 165 Dufferin Street
Toronto, Ontario, Canada M6K 3H6
Distributed in Great Britain and Europe by Chris Lloyd at Orca Book
Services, Stanley House, Fleets Lane, Poole BH15 3AJ, England
Distributed in Australia by Capricorn Link (Australia) Pty. Ltd.
P.O. Box 704, Windsor, NSW 2756, Australia

I'm Going To Read is a trademark of Sterling Publishing Co., Inc.

Sterling ISBN 1-4027-2713-5

ARE WE THERE YET?

Pictures by Dale Gottlieb

Sterling Publishing Co., Inc.
New York

Daddy kissed me good night.
He kissed my brother, too.

Daddy said, "Tomorrow we
will drive to a toy store in the city.
You can each pick one toy."

We went to sleep.
I dreamed about toys—
toys that whir and whiz
and beep and buzz.

My brother dreamed
about robots.

We wanted to get there,
so we rushed through breakfast.

"Don't eat so fast!"
said Daddy.

We ran to the car.

"How long will it take
to get there?" I asked.

"We'll be there in an hour,"
said Daddy.

We drove down a country road.

"ARE WE THERE YET?"

"Not yet," said Daddy.

We drove through
a dark tunnel.

"Not yet,"
said Daddy.

The car climbed a big hill.

"ARE WE THERE YET?"

"Not yet," said Daddy.

The car went around a curve.

"ARE WE THERE YET?"

"Not yet," said Daddy.

We stopped at a red light.

We crossed a small bridge.

"ARE WE
  THERE YET?"

"Ten more minutes,"
said Daddy.

"But you said that
ten minutes ago!" I yelled.

The car climbed another hill.
I could see the city.

We drove into town.

"WE'RE THERE!"

"We're at the toy store!"
said my brother.

We looked at a lot of toys—

toys that whir and whiz
and beep and buzz.

"We've been here a long time,"
said Daddy. "It's time to choose your toys."

And guess what? We did *not*
choose toys that whir and whiz
and beep and buzz.

I picked a pretty doll.
My brother picked a fuzzy bear.

"I'll pay for the toys,"
Daddy said. "Then we'll drive home."

"ARE WE THERE YET?"